HELLO, I'm THEA!

I'm *Geronimo Stilton*'s sister. As I'm sure you know from my brother's bestselling novels, I'm a special correspondent for *The Rodent's Gazette*, Mouse Island's most famouse newspaper. Unlike my 'fraidy mouse brother, I absolutely adore traveling, having adventures, and meeting rodents from all around the world!

The adventure I want to tell you about begins at Mouseford Academy, the school I went to when I was a young mouseling. I had such a great experience there as a student that I came back to teach a journalism class.

When I returned as a grown mouse, I met five really special students: Colette, Nicky, Pamela, Paulina, and Violet. You could hardly imagine five more different mouselings, but they became great friends right away. And they liked me so much that they decided to name their group after me: the Thea Sisters! I was so touched by that, I decided to write about their adventures. So turn the page to read a fabumouse adventure about the

THEA SISTERS!

colette

She has a passion for clothing and style, especially anything pink. When she grows up, she wants to be a fashion editor.

Paulina

Cheerful and kind, she loves traveling and meeting rodents from all over the world. She has a magic touch when it comes to technology.

violet

She's the bookworm of the group, and she loves learning. She enjoys classical music and dreams of becoming a famous violinist.

THE THEA SISTERS

Nicky

She comes from Australia and is very enthusiastic about sports and nature. She loves being outside and is always ready to get up and go!

Pamela

She is a great mechanic: Give her a screwdriver and she'll fix anything! She loves pizza, which she eats every day, and she loves to cook.

Do you want to help the Thea Sisters in this new adventure? It's not hard — just follow the clues!

When you see this magnifying glass, pay attention: It means there's an important clue on the page. Each time one appears, we'll review the clues so we don't miss anything.

**ARE YOU READY?
A NEW MYSTERY AWAITS!**

Geronimo Stilton

Thea Stilton
AND THE RIDDLE
OF THE RUINS

Scholastic Inc.

Published by Scholastic Inc., *Publishers since 1920*, 557 Broadway, New York, NY 10012. SCHOLASTIC and associated logos are trademarks and/or registered trademarks of Scholastic Inc.

Stilton is the name of a famous English cheese. It is a registered trademark of the Stilton Cheese Makers' Association. For more information, go to www.stiltoncheese.com.

This book is a work of fiction. Names, characters, places, and incidents are either the product of the author's imagination or are used fictitiously, and any resemblance to actual persons, living or dead, business establishments, events, or locales is entirely coincidental.

ISBN 978-1-338-26857-7

Text by Thea Stilton
Original title *Il tesoro scomparso*
Cover by Barbara Pellizzari, Giuseppe Facciotto, and Flavio Ferron
Illustrations by Barbara Pellizzari, Chiara Balleello, Valeria Cairoli, and Valentina Grassini
Graphics by Chiara Cebraro

Special thanks to AnnMarie Anderson
Translated by Andrea Schaffer
Interior design by Kay Petronio

10 9 8 7 6 5 4 3 2 1   18 19 20 21 22

Printed in the U.S.A.   40
First printing 2018

An Unexpected Prize

Most places on Whale Island are known for being beautiful and tranquil, but there's one EXCEPTION to the rule: **MOUSEFORD ACADEMY**! Students from all over the world come to study at the famous school, making it a lively, ENERGETIC, and not particularly quiet place.

Usually most students **LEAVE** campus for vacation in the summer. But this year was unusual: It was late June, and one classroom at Mouseford was still OVERFLOWING with mice!

"This archaeology seminar was a huge success!" Nicky commented as she looked around the room.

"I know," Paulina agreed, nodding. "I

didn't think there would be so **many** archaeology enthusiasts!"

Colette laughed. "If you ask me, I'd say some of the mice in this room are more *passionate* about the extra credit they'll get for attending the seminar than they are for ancient times," she said.

Her friends immediately knew who Colette was talking about: the Ruby Crew. They were sitting a few rows away, with their notebooks closed and **bored** expressions on their snouts.

Welcome!

"Luckily, today is the last day of this **torture**," the Thea Sisters heard Zoe tell her friends.

"I know," Ruby agreed eagerly. "The second this class is over, I'm hopping on my mother's yacht and sailing to a PRIVATE island. I'm spending the rest of the summer at a fabumouse **LUXURY** resort!"

At that moment, headmaster Octavius de Mousus cleared his throat and began to squeak.

"Students, during this summer course, you've worked hard and completed some **interesting** projects," he said proudly. "You've all done excellent work.

"The group of students who received the highest grade on the final project is Colette, Nicky, Paulina, Pamela, and Violet," he continued. "Their website dedicated to revealing the **history** of Whale Island was an **ENORMOUSE** success!"

Ruby rolled her eyes. "Does it really matter who got the highest grade?" she muttered to her friend Connie. "I mean, we all get extra credit just for taking this BORING class."

But the headmaster's next words knocked the grin right off Ruby's snout.

"I've also decided to award a special prize for the best project," he said. "These five students will have the opportunity to travel to Turkey for an **archaeological excavation** at Hierapolis!"

The Thea Sisters jumped to their paws: Had they understood correctly? Would they get to work with a REAL team of archaeologists?

"Sounds like a great prize," Ruby snickered.

"Who wants to spend her vacation working hard on a **dusty** old dig in the **hot** sun?"

"The archaeological site at Hierapolis is located near Pamukkale, a town famouse for its fascinating and beautiful travertine terraces and hot springs."

Ruby stopped squeaking immediately and regarded the Thea Sisters **enviously**.

At that moment, Professor Sparkle burst into the classroom.

"Please forgive the intrusion, Headmaster," he interrupted. "But I'm afraid there's a problem with the **reservations** for the students traveling to Turkey!"

The Thea Sisters glanced at one another: Was their dream going to be dashed so quickly? They had only just found about the **incredible** trip!

PACK YOUR BAGS!

The headmaster looked surprised.

"What's the problem?" he asked.

"Unfortunately, Professor Buruk and I had a misunderstanding," the history professor explained in a RUSH. "I thought the flight was scheduled for next week, but it turns out that it's really THIS AFTERNOON!"

The headmaster didn't flinch at the news. Instead, he turned to the Thea Sisters.

"I guess this means you five mice will have to pack your bags *quickly*," he said. "Come on, shake a paw and **get going**!"

The friends didn't make him repeat himself. They scampered out of the classroom **excitedly** and headed straight for their rooms.

"I can't believe this!" Nicky squeaked breathlessly. "We're really going to Turkey!"

"We'll need to bring **SUNSCREEN**, sunglasses, and **hats**." Colette began to list off items so the others wouldn't forget anything. "The sun is incredibly hot in Turkey at this time of year. And don't forget your swimsuits!"

"Coco, remember that we're going to Turkey to work on an archaeological dig," Violet pointed out practically. "We're not going on a relaxing *vacation*!"

"Exactly!" Pam agreed. "Make sure you all pack comfortable clothes, a few T-shirts, and a pair of **STURDY** shoes."

"You're right, of course, but I'm packing it anyway, just in case," Colette said with a smile. "When you go to a place with hot springs, it's always good to have a swimsuit!"

The group ended up following both friends' **advice**: They packed comfortable clothing as well as swimsuits and sun gear.

In a half hour, their bags were packed. The five mice were ready just in time, as Professor Sparkle appeared a few moments later to take them to the pier. There, a ferry would bring them to the mainland for their flight.

"First you'll fly to Istanbul," Professor Sparkle explained. "Then you'll take a second flight to Denizli, the city closest to the excavation site. My colleague and friend Professor Buruk has arranged for one of his students to GREET you when you arrive."

He gave the Thea Sisters their tickets and Professor Buruk's phone number. Then the five mice boarded the ferry, eager to begin a new adventure!

WELCOME
TO TURKEY

After traveling a long while, the Thea Sisters finally **LANDED** at a small, welcoming airport in Denizli.

"I wish we had had a chance to leave the airport in **ISTANBUL**," Paulina said wistfully.

"The place we are going is just as interesting," Pam reminded her friend. "I can't wait to see it!"

The Thea Sisters had left in such a hurry that they hadn't even had time to buy a tourist's **GUIDE** to visiting Turkey. Usually, when they traveled, the Thea Sisters liked to research the history and customs of their destination **before** the trip.

This time, it seemed they would discover everything day by day. Nicky was excited by that thought. Sometimes she had more 𝔣𝔲𝔫 when she didn't have anything planned!

Once the Thea Sisters got to the arrivals gate, they looked around.

"Professor Buruk's student must be here already," Colette said. "Keep an eye out for someone holding a sign with our names on it."

All around them, newly arrived passengers **hugged** family members and friends. A few drivers near the gate held up signs, but none had the Thea Sisters' names.

Tick, tock, tick, tock . . .

TEN minutes passed, and then another TEN.

The arrivals area emptied little by little.

"I'm starting to get worried," Violet told

her friends. "What if Professor Sparkle and Professor Buruk **MISUNDERSTOOD** each other about this detail, too?"

Nicky took out her **cell phone**.

"We can always call Professor Buruk," she reminded everyone. "We have his number. But first I really need some water. The plane made me so *thirsty*! Does anyone else want something?"

The others shook their heads, and Nicky went off. As soon as she found a newsstand, she bought a bottle of water, opened it, and took a big **GULP**. Satisfied, she scurried back toward her friends. But walking **QUICKLY** while drinking water in a crowded place wasn't the best idea.

Nicky tripped over someone's paw and fell to the ground in a small puddle of spilled water.

A mouse with **Dark eyes** sat sprawled on the ground next to her. Nicky had tripped over his paw, and her water had splashed all over his shirt.

"Oh, excuse me!" Nicky cried as she jumped to her paws and helped him up. "Are you okay? I should have paid more ATTENTION to where I was going."

"No, no, it was my **fault**," he replied apologetically as he smiled and accepted Nicky's help getting up.

"I'm sorry for bumping into you, but I'm terribly late! I'm here to **PICK UP** some people from the airport. But then there was a problem at the excavation and I couldn't find the keys to the **car**. And of course once I found the keys, the **traffic** driving to the airport was just terrible, and . . ."

"Excavation?" Nicky asked curiously.

"Yes, I'm working on the excavation site at **Hierapolis**," he replied. "Do you know about it? It's a **FASCINATING** job, but there are always so many things to do."

Nicky smiled.

"I understand," she said. "What's your name, and who are you here to pick up?"

"I'm Akhun and I am here to meet five mice from Mouseford Academy on Whale

Ooops!

It's okay . . .

Island," he replied. Then he looked around in alarm. "Where did my sign go?"

Nicky looked down at the ground. A PAPER with her and her friends' names on it was lying there, **soaking wet**.

"Oh no," Akhun groaned. "Now what do I do?"

Nicky just LAUGHED.

"Don't worry, you found us anyway," she reassured him. "My name is Nicky, and I'm one of the Mouseford students. Come on, I'll introduce you to my FRIENDS!"

COTTON CASTLE

The Thea Sisters and Akhun hit it off **immediately**.

"Our camp isn't too far from here," Akhun explained as he led the mouselets to the parking lot. "We'll DRIVE there in my minivan."

"I can't wait to get there!" Paulina replied. "None of us have ever been to a real excavation before. But I love archaeology."

"Have you been doing this work for long?" Violet asked him.

"I've been studying archaeology for **three years**," their guide replied. "And I've worked at the Hierapolis excavation with Professor Buruk for six months. How about you?"

"We actually just finished our first archaeology class," Nicky explained. "We're complete BEGINNERS!"

Akhun smiled encouragingly.

"You all seem very passionate about the subject, though," he said admiringly. "With enthusiasm and some hard work, your experience here will be truly **AMAZING**!"

Once they were in the minivan, Akhun began to tell the Thea Sisters about the place they were heading.

"*Pamukkale* means 'Cotton Castle,'" Akhun explained as he pointed proudly at the landscape outside the WINDOWS.

The Thea Sisters didn't respond. They

were stunned by the **breathtaking** landscape all around them.

It really seemed like they were surrounded by an expanse of white cotton.

"The *unique* look of the landscape here comes from the area's hot thermal waters, which are full of calcite," explained Akhun. "Over many centuries, this water has created mineral forests, petrified waterfalls, and natural pools in terraced basins."

The Thea Sisters looked out the windows, AMAZED. The landscape was like nothing they had ever seen before. It almost felt as if they were driving across the moon!

"Pamukkale and Hierapolis are both UNESCO World Heritage Sites," Akhun explained. "Look! You can see Hierapolis right in front of us!"

He pointed out the window at the ruins of an **ENORMOUSE** stone amphitheater encircled by the remains of **ancient** buildings.

"It's incredible!" Nicky exclaimed.

Akhun parked the minivan and helped the Thea Sisters *unload* their bags. Then he accompanied his new friends to the excavation's **BASE CAMP**, which was right near the ruins of the amphitheater. A large WHITE TENT served as headquarters for the team of professors and students working at the site.

"Hierapolis is more than two thousand years old," Akhun explained. "There's so much **history** here!"

The five mouselets stood outside the tent admiring the **ancient settlement**.

"If it looks like this now, imagine how **majestic** the amphitheater must have been years ago!" Colette whispered dreamily to her friends.

Humph!

"**EXCUSE ME!**" a sharp, unpleasant voice broke the silence. "Can you move? You five mice are just standing there with gaping snouts, and you're in my way."

The Thea Sisters

turned to see a mouse with shiny dark HAIR staring at them angrily.

She was pushing a wheelbarrow full of dirt and she seemed very ANNOYED.

"Wow, what an attitude!" Violet whispered.

Akhun just smiled and shrugged.

"Don't worry about Alya," he said. "That's just how she is. Now, come on. I want to introduce you to Professor Buruk!"

Akhun escorted the girls to the excavation

How exciting!

Welcome!

site, stopping at the edge of a **DEEP** hole in the earth.

"Professor!" Akhun called. "The Mouseford students are HERE!"

One of the **archaeologists** who was busy working on the dig raised his head. Then he climbed the walls of the excavation site and shook the paws of each of the mouselets, giving them a **large** smile.

"I am Professor Buruk," he said warmly.

"Welcome to Hierapolis. I'm so happy you're here. This will be a wonderful learning opportunity for all of you and for some of the mice here as well!"

He turned to the mouse with the dark hair and the surly look on her snout.

"Alya, please show the Thea Sisters to your BUNGALOW," he said. "They will stay with you."

"With me?!" she squeaked in disbelief. "All five? There isn't enough room. Plus, they brought enormouse suitcases!"

The Thea Sisters looked at their suitcases with a little embarrassment.

The professor smiled.

"What did I say?" he asked, sighing. "Everyone still has a Lot to learn . . ."

LET'S GET
TO WORK!

Alya **LED** the Thea Sisters to a small bungalow near the excavation site.

"Where can we put our things?" Colette asked cheerfully. She was trying to maintain a **FRIENDLY**, easygoing tone.

"Wherever you want, as long as you don't make a mess," Alya replied, **pointing** at the bunk beds. One of the beds was clearly hers, and the Thea Sisters claimed the rest of the beds while Alya left quickly.

"Well, we're not off to the **best** start," Pam commented, referring to Alya's rudeness.

"At least the professor seems **NICE**," Paulina said. "And this place is fantastic!"

Violet nodded enthusiastically. "It feels like

we've gone **back** in time," she said. "I can't wait to get started on the excavation."

"Me, too," Nicky agreed, arranging her things on the **TOP** level of one of the bunk beds.

When the Thea Sisters exited the bungalow, Akhun was waiting for them. He smiled and handed them bottles of **cold water**.

"Remember to drink a lot of water," he reminded them. "It's very **hot** on the site, and you don't want to get **DEHYDRATED**!"

Water?

Thanks!

Then Akhun took the Thea Sisters on a tour of the **EXCAVATION SITE**. He and Professor Buruk showed them how to use the various tools

What is an archaeological excavation?

An excavation is a controlled exploration of what lies beneath the earth. By digging in the soil and uncovering artifacts from ancient times, archaeologists can determine what types of human activities took place at the site in the past.

How does an excavation work?

Once archaeologists choose an area to study, the surface layer of grass and soil must be removed. To do this, archaeologists use tools such as spades, mattocks, shovels, and garden hoes.

Next, excavators dig using picks, blades, and trowels. Any artifacts that are revealed are documented and removed. Then they are gathered in bags and boxes and cataloged carefully. Any objects found are valuable, as they can help to explain how humans lived hundreds or thousands of years ago.

What does an archaeologist need on a dig site?

This depends on the location and climate of the excavation site, but excavators generally wear sturdy shoes, comfortable clothing, and a hat or helmet. Some other useful items include a medical kit, sunscreen, guidebook, notebook and pen, measuring tape, and a reusable water bottle.

on the site and introduced them to the other members of the FIELD TEAM.

"Excavation is a slow job," explained the professor. "The **dirt** is removed a little at a time to protect whatever is **HIDDEN** underneath.

"Here we find ourselves in front of a **GIGANTIC** archaeological treasure, but it isn't easy to extract the artifacts. Still, with careful and precise work, we can bring to **LIGHT** new discoveries regarding ancient civilizations!"

Professor Buruk led the Thea Sisters closer to the ancient structure that was half-buried in the earth.

"These are the remains of a house from the Byzantine Empire.* An ancient earthquake likely caused its **destruction**, and we are trying our best to **REBUILD** it."

---

*The ancient Greek city of Byzantium is now known as Istanbul.

"Excuse me, Professor," Violet interrupted. "Do you mean you want to RECONSTRUCT the building as if it had never crumbled?"

Buruk smiled.

"In a way, yes," he explained. "In situations like this one, we ARCHAEOLOGISTS can study the remains of the building and try to put all the ORIGINAL elements back together. But it's a very SLOW process. For now, we're simply uncovering and removing the first artifacts, which have been buried in the earth for well over a thousand years."

At this point, the professor had to excuse himself, and Akhun took over. He gave the Thea Sisters trowels and PAINTBRUSHES and explained their task in detail.

"We'll work on this part of the house first," he explained enthusiastically. "We believe this is the back of the house, and

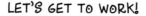
we've already discovered some small vases and parts of the wall."

The Thea Sisters watched Akhun work, taking note of his careful and methodical movements. When they felt ready, they began to work as well, following Akhun's instructions closely. **Slowly** but surely, they used their tools and paintbrushes to remove small bits of dirt and dust from the ancient STONE.

"Isn't this exciting?" Nicky asked as she brushed aside some dirt with her trowel. "I can't wait to uncover some IMPORTANT ARTIFACTS!"

A RELAXING SURPRISE

Two days later, Nicky wasn't quite as **ENTHUSIASTIC**, and neither were the other Thea Sisters.

"What's wrong?" Alya asked, observing their long snouts as they excavated. "Is the work **TOO HARD** for you?"

Sigh!

"No, it's not that," Paulina replied with a sigh.

Alya snickered.

"What is it, then?" she asked. "Do you miss your cool, comfortable beds and easy life at Mouseford Academy?"

Colette turned to face Alya.

"Mouseford is a school, not a luxury hotel," she said proudly. "We like to work hard. We just aren't used to the heat here."

"And it's a little **DISHEARTENING** that we haven't made much progress on the dig," Nicky explained. "We still haven't found **anything** . . ."

"Ah, you expected to make big discoveries?" Alya replied, laughing loudly.

"Please stop **TORMENTING** them," Akhun interrupted. "You were like that, too, when you first arrived, remember?"

What did you expect?

"Humph!" Alya said. "But I wasn't . . ."

"Alya!" Professor Buruk called suddenly. "I could use your help over here, **PLEASE**!"

Alya scurried over to the professor, and the Thea Sisters sighed with relief.

"What does she have **against** us?" Nicky asked Akhun. "I really don't know what we did to get on her bad side."

"Alya is slow to **warm up** to new mice," Akhun reassured her. "She just needs **time** to get used to having all of you here. And anyway, *I* like you."

Nicky **blushed**, and Akhun found himself stuttering in reply.

"I m-mean, it's just, well —"

"**LOOK!**" exclaimed Colette, interrupting him.

Professor Buruk had revealed a huge object in the earth: It was a large capital* that had been **PRESERVED** almost perfectly!

Wow!

*A capital is an architectural element found at the top of a column. Turn to page 54 to learn more.

"How wonderful!" Nicky said excitedly.

The capital was cleaned and cataloged, and the Thea Sisters had the honor of watching the work closely. By the time the team was done, it was almost the end of the Thea Sisters' shift. The sun was high in the sky and it was very hot.

"I know the perfect way to celebrate our latest discovery," Professor Buruk said with a sly wink at Akhun.

"LET'S GO SWIMMING!" Akhun exclaimed.

The professor smiled and nodded.

"Thanks, Professor," Akhun said happily. "You're the BEST!"

The Thea Sisters headed back to the bungalow to change into their swimsuits. Then Professor Buruk drove the team to the area's hot springs, where tourists were relaxing in the white pools of thermal water.

Paulina dipped one paw into the water and drew it out, a PUZZLED look on her snout.

Let's go swimming!

"But . . . the water is **hot**!" she exclaimed. "And it seems **fizzy**!"

"Well, it *is* a hot spring," Alya replied drily.

"Give it a chance," Akhun said with a smile. "I think you are going to LIKE it. This area is crowded with tourists, but after our swim, I can show you a few natural pools that are even more beautiful."

Once they became used to the warm water, the Thea Sisters were able to relax and enjoy themselves. After their swim, they got dressed and **followed** Akhun along a

narrow trail that led to an area that was free of crowds. There they were able to admire the incredible landscape and SNAP some photos.

"What an amazing place!" Colette exclaimed as she took in the incredible sunset.

Her friends were also enchanted by the spectacular landscape. They enjoyed the view and they forgot all about the **exhaustion** and discomfort of the archaeological excavation. When they finally headed back to the dig site, they felt REFRESHED and iNViGORateD!

AN UNEXPECTED ARRIVAL

In the next few days, the **excavators** unearthed a few more items, including a *second* capital. One afternoon, Professor Buruk's team was working hard to carefully **REMOVE** the capital from the earth when a **cloud** of dust rose in the distance.

"What's that?" Colette asked as she pushed her wide-brimmed **HAT** back so she could see better. A moment later, an SUV emerged from the **DUST**.

"It's probably a group of **tourists**," Akhun said with a shrug.

But as Professor Buruk's team watched, three mice climbed out of the car and began **unloading** archaeological tools.

"Good morning," the tallest mouse said in a not particularly **friendly** voice. "Who's in charge here?"

Professor Buruk was lying on the ground, carefully dusting off a small portion of what remained of a wall of an ancient building. He slowly rose and brushed himself off before approaching the new arrivals.

"Good morning," he replied, sticking out his paw politely. "I'm Professor Buruk."

"I am Professor Brenninger," the tall mouse said. "These are my assistants, Carl and Sandra."

"It's nice to meet you," Professor Buruk said. "I'm sorry . . . we weren't expecting another team on the site."

"Oh, that's too bad," Professor Brenninger replied. "It seems our universities didn't understand each other. I hope it won't be a problem for you to have us working on the excavation as well."

"Not at all," said Buruk with a smile. "Surely you know Professor Brown; I met him many years ago at a convention. He's a great scholar and archaeologist. If you see him, please say hello for me."

"Of course," Professor Brenninger said. "Now, if you'll excuse me, we must get to work. We don't have any time to lose!"

Professor Buruk seemed taken aback by Professor Brenninger's abrupt dismissal, but he remained cordial.

"Good luck, then," Professor Buruk said.

The new arrivals immediately began to set up a small archaeological worksite just a short distance from Professor Buruk's team.

"What a strange mouse," Nicky observed.

"Maybe he thinks he is smarter than we are. I hear he comes from a very *prestigious* university," Akhun said with a shrug. "I've met similar mice before."

"Well, you don't have to go to a prestigious university to be a good archaeologist," Nicky said firmly. "Hard work and dedication are the keys to success!"

Akhun smiled at Nicky, **THANKFUL** for her support. Then they both returned to the excavation.

Professor Brenninger and his assistants began their work as well. Soon the Thea Sisters were **absorbed** in the task at hand and had forgotten all about the newcomers.

NOT-SO-FRIENDLY NEIGHBORS

The next day, it was clear that Professor Brenninger's assistants hadn't worn enough sunscreen the previous day: They both had badly **sunburned** snouts, and they had tied their shirts around their heads to protect themselves from further damage.

"That's odd," Nicky remarked. "They acted so experienced, I expected them to pay more attention to a detail like that!"

Colette pulled a tube of sunscreen out of her pocket.

"Maybe I should offer them some sunscreen before they're completely roasted!" she said generously.

"Good idea, Coco!" Paulina agreed.

Get out of here!

Go away!

The two **friends** approached Carl and Sandra.

"It looks like you stayed out in the sun too long yesterday," Colette said **sympathetically**. "Would you like some sunscreen? I brought plenty!"

But the **archaeologists' reaction** wasn't exactly what Colette expected.

"Get out of here!" Sandra squeaked angrily.

"Yes, **GO BACK** to your excavation, spies!" Carl added.

"Whoa!" Colette replied. "I was just trying to help."

Professor Brenninger had been **relaxing** under a white tent when he noticed the commotion and approached the four mice.

"What's going on here?" he asked **MENACINGLY**. "Is there a problem?"

"Let's go, Colette," Paulina replied quickly, shaking her head. "They clearly don't **NEED** or **want** our help."

The two friends returned to Pam, Nicky, Violet, and Akhun feeling confused by the **unfriendly** reception they had received.

"Well, they didn't want any sunscreen," Colette explained.

"And they were really **rude** about it, too," Paulina added, a puzzled look on her snout.

"Maybe they were **embarrassed**," Akhun offered. "After all, they should have been more responsible about wearing hats and sunscreen yesterday!"

"That's true," Colette said. "But they were

more **suspicious** of us than embarrassed, I think."

Paulina nodded. "It was very strange," she agreed.

Nicky had been busy digging while the others discussed the strange interaction. But she stopped working SUDDENLY. Her trowel had hit something hard, and she quickly brushed some dirt aside with her paintbrush.

"Akhun!" she said excitedly. "Take a look at this. I may be wrong, but I think we may have found SOMETHING . . ."

Akhun hurried over to take a look. He bent down and carefully brushed off more dirt with his paw.

"You're right!" he exclaimed. "It looks like an amphora! That's a type of pottery that was used in ancient times to store liquids or grains. Help me pull it out!"

An important Discovery

Alya glared at the Thea Sisters enviously when she saw the amphora that Nicky and Akhun had removed from the DIRT.

"Humph!" she muttered. "Beginner's luck!"

But she was the only one who wasn't happy: All the other archaeologists and assistants complimented Nicky.

"It's a special day: You found your very first **ancient artifact**!" Professor Buruk said. "Archaeology connects us to the past and to the history of those who came long before us. I'm sure **MEMORIES** of this moment will remain with you forever!"

Nicky smiled and admired the amphora. There was one small **chip** on the edge, but the rest of the vessel was completely intact.

"Thanks, Akhun!" Nicky told her new friend excitedly. "I couldn't have done it **without you**!"

Akhun blushed when he felt everyone's eyes on him.

"Great job, both of you," Professor Buruk said. "Excellent teamwork, right, Alya?"

The mouselet scowled at the professor, crossing her arms across her chest.

The Thea Sisters helped *catalog* the amphora, and then they returned to work.

Pamela, Colette, Nicky, and Paulina threw themselves into their work eagerly, full of enthusiasm.

"That was so exciting," Pam chattered. "I can't wait to find another artifact!"

But Violet hadn't squeaked a word.

"Vi, what's wrong?" Colette asked.

"Do you need to take a break for a drink of water?"

"No, thanks, I'm fine," Violet replied **DistracteDly**, looking at Professor Brenninger's excavation.

The others turned to look as well.

Professor Brenninger was relaxing in his chair in the shade, snoring peacefully. Meanwhile, his assistants were sweating and toiling away under the boiling sun.

"How odd," Violet observed, shaking her snout in disbelief. "You would think the professor would want to be awake to zzz··· help with his team's excavation."

"Maybe archaeologists who work for prestigious universities leave the HARD WORK to their assistants!" Akhun snickered.

"Well, I much prefer working for Professor Buruk," Nicky said warmly. She gestured to the professor, who was kneeling on the ground, carefully brushing the capital, his BEARD white with dust.

Her friends nodded and went back to work. But Professor Brenninger's team's strange habits didn't STOP there.

Violet was keeping an eye on them as she worked, so she happened to overhear a bizarre conversation between Carl and Sandra.

"Just wait until we find what we're looking for," Carl murmured. "It will be so embarrassing for them!"

"Yeah," Sandra replied, laughing. "Their discovery of that silly amphora and a crumbling Corinthian capital will pale in comparison to ours!"

Violet reported the conversation back to her friends.

"They've got some nerve to brag about a discovery before they've even made it," Nicky said in surprise.

Akhun was perplexed.

"Did they really refer to it as a **CORINTHIAN** capital?" he asked.

"Yes," Violet replied. "That's what they said."

"I don't understand," Akhun continued. "They can't be telling the TRUTH about their training, then."

"What makes you say that?" Violet asked in *alarm*.

"Because the column Professor Buruk found was an IONIC column," Akhun explained. "Any archaeology student would know that!"

CAPITAL CONUNDRUM

CAPITAL: AN ARCHITECTURAL ELEMENT AT THE TOP OF A BUILDING'S COLUMN.

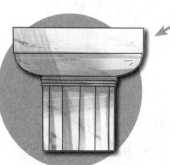

DORIC CAPITAL: THE SIMPLEST DESIGN.

IONIC CAPITAL: DECORATED WITH TWO SPIRAL SCROLLS, CALLED *VOLUTES*.

CORINTHIAN CAPITAL: THE MOST ELEGANT DESIGN, IT IS DECORATED WITH CARVED LEAVES AND VOLUTES.

EVERYONE TO ¡STANBUL!

The next day, Professor Buruk's team had planned a well-deserved day off. As a special treat, the professor had offered to take everyone to Istanbul for a day of sightseeing.

"This way our friends from Mouseford will have a chance to see one of the most beautiful cities in the world," Professor Buruk had said proudly.

Everyone was so busy preparing for the trip that Akhun and the Thea Sisters forgot all about Professor Brenninger's team and their suspicious behavior.

After an hour-long flight from Denizli, the group landed in Istanbul.

"Where do we begin?" Nicky asked enthusiastically, once she and the Thea Sisters had made their way from the airport to the center of town. She and her friends were surrounded by ancient monuments, green spaces, and wide streets.

Follow me!

"Well, today you'll have an exceptional **G·U·I·D·E**!" Akhun exclaimed. "I'm from Istanbul; I was born and raised here. I actually became **passionate** about archaeology thanks to the history that is alive in every corner of this beautiful city. First, let's head to my favorite place!"

Akhun led them to a small, building that seemed quite **ordinary**.

But when the Thea Sisters followed him down a flight of stairs, they found themselves in an **EXTRAORDINARY** place beneath the rest of the city.

"Welcome to the Basilica Cistern!" Akhun said proudly.

Dozens of very tall columns held up a vaulted ceiling, and a **footbridge** allowed visitors to walk above what seemed like a large subterranean **LAKE**.

"There are even fish!" Paulina exclaimed, pointing at the water.

"Yes!" Akhun said enthusiastically. "This underground chamber was built in 532 CE and was used to hold fresh water for the buildings nearby. But the most interesting thing about it is that its existence was *forgotten* for many centuries!

"Then, in the 1500s, a traveler heard stories that some of the city's inhabitants got fresh water — and even **fish** — from

holes in the floors of their basements. The cistern was soon rediscovered!"

"What a fascinating story!" Nicky said breathlessly.

Akhun smiled.

"The first time I came down here on an elementary school field trip, I knew that I would be an archaeologist when I GREW UP."

After bombarding Akhun with questions and taking dozens of PHOTOS, the Thea Sisters emerged from the cistern. From there, Akhun led them on a tour of the city's most famouse monuments, including the Topkapi Palace Museum, a former imperial palace that contains many ancient treasures.

"Anyone getting hungry?" Akhun asked his friends after the museum tour.

"Yes!" Pamela exclaimed eagerly. "I could eat an entire cheese pizza by myself!"

"How about a quick stop for some FALAFEL SANDWICHES, then?" Akhun asked.

"Sounds great," Nicky replied, "but what's falafel?"

"You'll love it," Akhun reassured her. "Falafel are fried fritters made from chickpeas and vegetables. They are served in pita bread with garlic or yogurt sauce."

After a delicious and filling lunch, Akhun led his friends to an ENORMOUSE indoor market.

Colette was delighted.

"Are we going shopping?" she asked.

"Of course!" Akhun replied with a laugh. "You can't visit Istanbul without a stop at the Grand Bazaar, one of the world's oldest and LARGEST covered markets."

The Thea Sisters wandered happily from

one stall to the next, admiring everything from soft silk scarves to sparkling jewelry. There were candy stalls and stalls filled with aromatic spices, and the five friends had FUN exploring, tasting, wearing, and observing everything.

At the END of the day, the group headed to the airport with a few extra accessories

and a box of *lokum* — delicate candies covered in sugar, also called Turkish delight.

By the time they arrived back in Hierapolis, it was already **DARK**. The Thea Sisters' hearts were full of memories of their special trip, but they were also *exhausted*. Within minutes of changing into their pajamas and climbing into their bunks, all five mice were soon fast asleep.

AN UNPLEASANT SURPRISE

The next morning, Pam awoke to the ringing sound of her alarm clock.

"I slept like a **ROCK**!" she proclaimed happily.

"Me, too!" Paulina agreed.

Colette and Nicky had also slept **SOUNDLY**, and Alya was snoring softly in her bunk.

"Violet?" Nicky asked as she leaned over to see her friend **sleeping** on the bunk below her.

There was a muffled groan, and then Violet's snout emerged from under the sheets, her fur rumpled and MESSY.

I'm so sleepy!

"Lucky you!" she said sleepily.

"I slept terribly! Loud sounds outside kept waking me up!"

"Loud sounds?" Colette asked. "I didn't hear a thing."

"I didn't hear **ANYTHING**, either," Nicky said, and the others nodded in agreement.

"Alya, did you hear something?" Violet asked.

But Alya just grunted and rolled over.

"Could it have been a dream?" Nicky wondered.

"No," Violet replied, shaking her head. "I'm sure of what I heard. Something woke me, and I wasn't able to fall back to sleep. You mice know I'm a grumpy mess when I don't sleep well. Today's going to be a rough day!"

When the Thea Sisters dressed and left the

bungalow, they discovered that Violet had been *right*. Something certainly had happened the previous **NIGHT**. Professor Buruk was looking at the excavation grimly. The capital he had discovered and **extracted** with so much care was buried back under a thick layer of dirt! And next to it there was a **broken** wheelbarrow.

"How could this have happened?" Akhun asked.

The Thea Sisters immediately looked around, searching for **clues**, but the pawprints of the team covered the tracks. "It looks like **sabotage**!" Alya exclaimed angrily.

But Professor Buruk had another thought.

"Let's not jump to conclusions," he said cautiously. "It could have been an animal. The other day I saw a dog sniffing around the 𝕒𝕟𝕔𝕚𝕖𝕟𝕥 𝕥𝕙𝕖𝕒𝕥𝕖𝕣.* Maybe it came over here to play and ruined the wheelbarrow and piled up the dirt."

"Hmmm," Alya replied, her lips tight. She looked UNCONVINCED, and this time the Thea Sisters agreed with her.

Suddenly, Professor Brenninger appeared.

"What happened?" he asked.

"Oh, **NOTHING**," Professor Buruk responded calmly. "Just a small nocturnal INCIDENT."

Professor Brenninger narrowed his eyes at Buruk.

"Some of our *tools* have disappeared," he said accusingly. "Do you know anything about it?"

"No, I'm sorry," Professor Buruk replied in surprise.

The Thea Sisters moved away from the

---

*The ancient theater at Hierapolis was built in the second century CE under the Roman Emperor Hadrian.

others and began to talk quietly among themselves.

"Did you hear that?" Colette whispered. "Something strange happened to Professor Brenninger's team, too!"

"So maybe there really is a **SABOTEUR**!" Pam exclaimed.

CLUES!

WHAT COULD HAVE HAPPENED AT THE CAMP?

DID AN ANIMAL REALLY MOVE THE DIRT AND BREAK THE WHEELBARROW?

WHO TOOK PROFESSOR BRENNINGER'S TEAM'S TOOLS?

"Or maybe Professor Buruk is right, and an animal did it by mistake," offered Paulina.

Nicky sighed.

"Whatever it is, the only thing we can do is get back to work!" she said.

The team spent the morning CLEANING UP the excavation site. Professor Buruk got everyone involved, and the mice worked in a LINE, passing the dirt from one mouse

What do you think?

It's incredible!

to the next until the column reemerged in the light of the sun.

Everyone stopped for a moment to celebrate by breaking into a round of *applause*.

"Time for a break!" Professor Buruk exclaimed happily. "Thank you all for your hard work."

Nicky decided to take advantage of the break to see the **ancient theater** near the excavation site up close. The amphitheater was a truly impressive structure, with rows and rows of marble seats arranged in a semicircle.

"It's incredible to think that this was here two thousand years ago," said a voice behind her.

It was Akhun. He handed her a cold drink and admired the amphitheater with her.

"It makes me feel very, very small, but also

connected to ancient history," Akhun explained thoughtfully. "It's amazing to think of all those who existed before us and all those who will come after us, isn't it? Someday I hope to have a job just like Professor Buruk's."

Nicky smiled.

"Your passion for ancient history is *contagious*," she replied warmly. "I'm sure you'll be a great archaeologist someday."

"Thank you," Akhun replied SHYLY.

Thank you!

Just believe in yourself!

"Sometimes I worry that I don't have the right **character** for it. Alya is much more decisive than me, for example."

Nicky was quiet for a moment, trying to find the right words to **ENCOURAGE** her friend.

"But you're a real **team player**," Nicky pointed out. "That's very important, especially in this field — even Professor Buruk says so! You just need to **believe in yourself!**"

Akhun smiled at his friend.

"You're right, Nicky," he replied. "Thank you for the pep talk. I'm so glad I met you. I really appreciate your **friendship!**"

"Speaking of friendship, we'd better get back to the Thea Sisters," Nicky said. "The **excavation** awaits!"

TOOL TROUBLE

The next morning, the Thea Sisters were enjoying a *cheerful*, relaxing meal with the group.

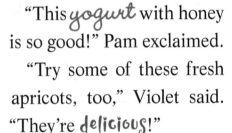

"This *yogurt* with honey is so good!" Pam exclaimed.

"Try some of these fresh apricots, too," Violet said. "They're *delicious!*"

Luckily, Violet had slept well and was feeling **refreshed** after the previous sleepless night.

"The next few days will be EXCITING!" Akhun said, his eyes shining. "We'll finally be able to see the walls of the building we're excavating."

"That's right," Professor Buruk confirmed.

"In fact, I'd like to take some photos this morning to track our progress so far. We can even get a **group photo** of the entire team! Akhun, would you be able to get the camera once you're done with breakfast?"

"Of course, Professor!" Akhun replied eagerly.

Professor Buruk gave Akhun the key to the equipment shed where the tools and instruments for the expedition were stored.

A few minutes passed, but Akhun hadn't returned.

"Why is it taking So long?" Alya huffed impatiently. "How long does it take to FIND a camera?"

"Alya . . ." Professor Buruk warned, giving her a serious look.

"I'll go SEE if he needs help," Nicky offered. The professor nodded at her.

Nicky hurried to the shed and poked her head in.

"Akhun, is everything all right?" she asked.

But she knew the answer as soon as she saw the interior of the shed. It was a complete **MESS**!

"The camera's gone!" Akhun exclaimed. "And it's not the only thing that's **MISSING**!"

Nicky looked around in concern. Someone had clearly rummaged through everything in the shed.

"Entire boxes of tools are gone," Akhun moaned. "And the ground-penetrating radar has disappeared, too!"

"What's that?" Nicky asked.

"A GPR device uses ELECTROMAGNETIC WAVES to help us determine what's under the earth before we start to dig," Akhun explained quickly. "It's one of the most

IMPORTANT tools on an archaeological expedition site — and it's very expensive!"

"Are you sure it was in HERE?" Nicky asked. "Maybe someone moved it."

"No, Professor Buruk is very clear about our tools and equipment," Akhun explained. "All the materials and instruments are locked in here when not in use, and you need a key to open the shed."

Nicky LOOKED around.

"Hmmm," she wondered. "How did the objects disappear if the door was locked?"

She looked around the shed more closely and saw the answer immediately: A window just over some of the shelves was wide-open.

"How did that happen?" Nicky exclaimed.

It was now clear to both mice that someone had broken into the shed to steal the tools.

Nicky and Akhun quickly returned to the group and let them know what had happened. Professor Buruk was very UPSET.

"The GPR device was stolen?!" he exclaimed worriedly. "That's a huge setback!"

"Did you look around carefully?" Alya asked in an accusatory tone. "You seem to have trouble finding things a lot, Akhun."

"The window was forced open!"

Akhun replied defensively. "It's not my fault. Why are you trying to make me look bad?"

"I don't need to make you look bad," Alya replied. "You do it **VERY WELL** by yourself!"

"Please, stop it," Professor Buruk said. "Haven't I explained a thousand times that **archaeology** is a team effort?"

Alya and Akhun bowed their heads, ashamed at their outbursts.

"What do we do now, Professor?" asked another assistant.

"We could go talk to Professor Brenninger," Nicky interjected quickly. "Maybe he or one of his assistants saw something."

Did you look closely?

It's not my fault!

"That seems like a good idea," replied Professor Buruk. "We

can also ask them if they can loan us some instruments."

"Let's hope Professor Brenninger and his team are a little friendlier than they've been so far," Violet remarked.

"I'm sure they'll lend a helping paw once they realize what's happened," Paulina said optimistically. "After all, archaeology is a team effort, right?"

CLUES!

WHO BROKE INTO PROFESSOR BURUK'S SHED?

IS THE THEFT RELATED TO THE BROKEN WHEELBARROW AND THE BURIED ARTIFACT?

WHAT DOES THIS HAVE TO DO WITH PROFESSOR BRENNINGER'S TEAM'S MISSING TOOLS?

LOST AND FOUND

Unfortunately, Professor Brenninger was as unfriendly as usual.

"I don't see how your problem affects us," he told Professor Buruk. "We certainly didn't take your tools."

"No, no, of course not!" Professor Buruk reassured him hurriedly. "We're not accusing you. We just wanted to let you know what happened and ask if you or your assistants saw anything unusual last night or this morning."

"We didn't SEE or HEAR anything," Carl said. "In fact,

We don't know anything!

some of our tools went **missing** yesterday."

"That's right," Sandra added, *crossing* her arms across her chest defensively. "We don't know anything about it!"

"Try to think *carefully*," Professor Buruk persisted. "Even a tiny detail could help —"

"**I'm sorry**, but we didn't see anything," Professor Brenninger said, cutting him off.

Nicky took a **DEEP** breath.

"Speaking of equipment, would you happen to have anything we can **borrow**?" she inquired politely. "We would take **EXCELLENT** care of everything!"

Professor Brenninger scowled. Nicky figured he was about to say no, but then he shrugged.

"If it means that much to you, you can **borrow** some tools," he said gruffly. "Only a few items were taken yesterday."

Then he led them to his team's equipment tent. There were piles of paintbrushes, picks, rakes, and buckets everywhere.

"What a mess!" Colette whispered to her friends.

Even Professor Buruk seemed surprised at the disarray in the tent.

"Did this all happen to your tent yesterday?" he said worriedly.

"No, no," Professor Brenninger replied dismissively. "This is all Carl. He's very disorganized."

Professor Buruk and his team chose a few instruments, and then Professor Brenninger quickly hustled them out of the tent.

"Those three mice act very strangely," Violet commented.

Akhun nodded.

"And did you see all that stuff in their tent?" Akhun added. "Those were very old tools. They must have raided the bottom of their **archaeology** department's closet!"

"But I thought they worked for a really prestigious university," Nicky remarked, a **confused** look on her snout.

"Hey, there's no time for chitchat," Alya squeaked suddenly, interrupting them. "We need to find our tools! Or, at the very least, we could use some **CLUES** as to where they disappeared to."

So Professor Buruk's team spent the rest of the day searching the entire excavation site.

It seemed as though the day's searching had been in vain, when Nicky made a sudden *discovery* late in the afternoon. She was standing near a tower next to a majestic colonnade as the sun set, creating a very LONG shadow.

Nicky was admiring the beautiful scenery for a moment when she tripped over a small, tapered object. She looked down and saw a SCALPEL under her paw. Nicky picked it up and looked around to see where it had come from, but there did not seem to be any other equipment or excavation area in SIGHT.

What's this?

Then she glanced around and noticed that the tower had a DOOR. Cautiously, Nicky approached the tower and peeked inside. What she saw inside left her momentarily squeakless!

An incredible Discovery

Once she got over her **SHOCK**, Nicky ran back to camp to find the others.

"Come take a look," she said quickly.

Professor Buruk's team hurried after her. When they got to the tower, they discovered all their tools and instruments had been **PACKED** inside.

"**WHAT LUCK!**" Professor Buruk exclaimed as he examined the precious GPR device. "I don't think it's *damaged*."

"The rest of the equipment looks fine, too," Alya confirmed. "Nothing's **BROKEN**."

"It's so strange, though," Akhun said, perplexed. "Who could have done something like this?"

"Maybe the thief realized he wasn't going to get away with it, and he abandoned everything in the first place he found," Pam suggested.

"Well, the important thing is that we can return to work tomorrow," Professor Buruk said happily. "What a relief!"

"Yes, hopefully we can relax a bit now that we've found the tools," Colette agreed.

But Colette had squeaked too soon. As soon as the team had returned all the tools and equipment to Professor Buruk's shed, an SUV pulled up to the site. Curious, the Thea Sisters headed over to see who was inside. Professor Buruk and his assistants followed.

The group watched as two mice with suitcases climbed out of the car and headed straight for Professor Brenninger's camp.

"Other **archaeologists**?" Nicky guessed.

But when the newcomers pulled out a video camera and microphones, Pamela had a different thought.

"They look more like journalists to me," she remarked.

Meanwhile, Professor Brenninger was busy brushing the dust off his clothing and combing his **fur**. When he realized Professor Buruk's team was watching, he flashed them a large smile.

"It's your **lucky day**, Buruk!" he exclaimed loudly. "You'll be able to tell others that you were here when I revealed my big discovery!"

Professor Brenninger stepped right up to the microphone and pointed at an object covered by a **SHeet**.

"Be sure to *zoom in* on that one," he

instructed the cameramouse. "It's my great discovery!"

Then Professor Brenninger squeaked for a long time about the significance of his **archaeological work**. Finally, he pulled back the sheet.

Professor Brenninger had discovered two clay **STATUES** sitting on thrones. They were beautifully carved and in **excellent** condition.

Professor Buruk and his team listened to the entire interview before the professor finally motioned for everyone to RETURN to their base camp.

"Let Professor Brenninger enjoy his moment of glory and celebrate with his team," Professor Buruk said generously. "Tomorrow we can **ask** him to show us his discovery. We'll be among the first in the archaeological world to examine those statues up close!"

But Akhun wasn't feeling so generous.

"It isn't **FAIR**!" he grumbled. "We excavate for months, then Brenninger arrives and in just a few days his team makes an **incredible discovery**!"

Professor Buruk smiled affectionately.

"Try not to be discouraged, Akhun," he said. "You're still very young. An archaeologist's career consists of **HARD WORK**, a lot of waiting, and a pinch of luck."

Despite Professor Buruk's pep talk, Akhun still seemed glum. Nicky was about to try to cheer him up when Professor Brenninger's assistant Sandra arrived.

"Professor Brenninger would like to invite you all for dinner tonight to celebrate his **exceptional** discovery," she said simply.

Then she turned and left without waiting for a reply.

CELEBRATION AND MYSTERY

The Thea Sisters headed to their bungalow to get dressed for dinner. Alya was there, too, **struggling** to put her hair up in a bun at the top of her head.

After a moment of hesitation, Colette approached her.

"If I were you, I would leave it down," she suggested in a friendly voice. "You have *beautiful* hair!"

At first it seemed Alya was going to respond with a **rude** remark. But then the look on her snout SOFTENED.

"Do you think so?" she asked as she glanced in the mirror. "Maybe you're right."

Once they were ready, the Thea Sisters and

Alya met up with Professor Buruk. He was elegantly dressed in a cream-colored linen suit. Meanwhile, Professor Brenninger had donned a crisp white suit with a **bright red** handkerchief tucked in his pocket. His happiness at his discovery had transformed him into a different mouse.

He no longer seemed *arrogant* or aloof. Instead, he seemed intent on enjoying the company of the same mice he had brushed off just days before.

"He seems much more relaxed since his discovery, doesn't he?" Pam remarked.

"Maybe he was rude earlier because he was AFRAID he wouldn't find anything," Violet suggested. "Now that the pressure is off, he seems friendlier."

Professor Brenninger brought everyone to a RESTAURANT in Pamukkale. When they entered, it seemed to the Thea Sisters that they were entering a fairy tale. There were PLUSH carpets, chairs with DECORATIVE pillows, and LARGE chandeliers everywhere, creating a unique and magical atmosphere.

"Smell that aroma!" Pam exclaimed enthusiastically. "It smells delicious. I almost haven't missed pizza since I've been in Turkey."

Her friends laughed. They all knew how

much Pam loved pizza. She would miss it no matter how **amazing** the local cuisine was!

They sat down and were about to begin eating some delicious-looking pastry filled with spinach and feta cheese called *gozleme*.

But, suddenly, Nicky realized someone was

missing. She hadn't seen **Akhun** yet.

"Maybe he went to *wash* his paws before the meal," Colette suggested.

But a quick **SURVEY** revealed that no one had seen him.

For some reason, Akhun *wasn't there* with the rest of his team.

WHERE IS AKHUN?

The Thea Sisters told Professor Buruk that they were worried about their friend's absence.

"I'm sure he's **fine**," Professor Buruk said. "I know he was feeling a little down, so maybe he didn't feel like celebrating. He probably stayed at the site and grabbed a quick dinner there."

"Yes, you're probably right," Nicky replied, but she still felt uneasy. She felt badly that she hadn't noticed his absence sooner!

Professor Buruk could tell Nicky was still worried about Akhun.

"Why don't I try calling him?" the professor offered.

"Yes, PLEASE!" Nicky agreed eagerly.

Professor Buruk took out his cell phone and dialed the number, but unfortunately there was **NO ANSWER**.

"What if something happened to him?" Nicky asked worriedly.

"Maybe he went for a walk and left his phone behind," Professor Buruk said. "Akhun is a very responsible mouse."

Don't worry, Nicky!

Meanwhile, the other dinner guests were applauding the professor. He had just announced that he was planning a press conference for the next evening in Denizli to officially announce his discovery.

But Nicky couldn't focus on anything but **Akhun**. Even though she hadn't known him long, she knew it wasn't like him to disappear without telling anyone.

When they went back to the camp, the Thea Sisters **hurried** to Akhun's bungalow. His roommates didn't seem worried. They assumed he was **asleep** in his room. But when the Thea Sisters knocked on his door, there was no answer. Finally, they peeked inside, but they didn't find any trace of their friend.

"Maybe he's taking a **walk**," suggested Kamil, one of the young archaeologists on the team. "Sometimes he likes to walk through the **ruins** of Hierapolis."

"He couldn't have gone **very** far," Colette pointed out. "All his things are still **HERE**."

"I'm sure you're right," Nicky said reluctantly. "I'm probably making SOMETHING out of NOTHING."

So the Thea Sisters returned to their bungalow.

"Akhun does this sometimes," Alya remarked. "He probably went out for a walk and was LATE getting back for dinner. When he realized we had left without him, he was probably embarrassed and he didn't want to be here when we got back."

Nicky GLARED at her.

"Why do you always have to put him down, Alya?" she asked.

"I'm not putting him down," responded Alya defensively. "I'm just saying that's what probably happened."

Nicky went to sleep in a **bad mood**. She tossed and turned all night and didn't feel much better when she woke in the morning.

She jumped out of bed and got dressed

immediately. Then she headed to the canteen for **BREAKFAST**, hoping to bump into Akhun on the way.

But when she got there, the first mouse she saw was Kamil, not Akhun. He looked worried.

"You were right, Nicky," he said. "Akhun didn't **COME BACK** to the bungalow last night!"

Nicky jumped up.

"We have to tell Professor

Akhun didn't come back!

What?!

Buruk!" she said quickly. "And then we're going to search until we find him!"

At that moment, Colette, Pam, Paulina, and Violet headed over to join Nicky and Kamil.

"What happened?" Colette asked when she saw the concerned look on Nicky's snout.

"Akhun didn't **COME BACK** to his bungalow last night," she replied.

"Oh no!" Paulina exclaimed. "We have to tell the professor right away!"

Professor Buruk emerged from his bungalow at that moment, holding a cup of tea.

"What do you need to tell me?" he asked.

"Akhun is missing!" Nicky cried.

The professor smiled.

"Don't worry," he said. "Your friend is fine. He sent me a **message** last night to let me know that his father fell off his bike and ḥüṙṫ his leg. Akhun had to return to Istanbul for a few days to lend his father a paw until he **GetS Better**."

The professor held out his cell phone and showed the Thea Sisters the message from Akhun.

Professor Buruk,
My father had a bicycle accident, so I'm going back to Istanbul for a few days. It's nothing serious, so don't worry.
See you soon,
Akhun

"But he didn't take **any** of his things!" Nicky replied. "His suitcase is still in the bungalow."

The professor paused for a moment.

"Okay, here's an **idea**," he said at last. "I was planning to give everyone a DAY OFF today anyway. I can give you Akhun's phone number and address in Istanbul, and you can **call him** or VISIT him if you like."

TRACES OF AKHUN

Nicky tried calling Akhun, but he didn't answer.

"It's too bad the professor didn't have his HOME NUMBER," Violet said.

"What should we do?" Paulina asked. "Do you think we should go to Istanbul to look for him?"

"First, we should ask around at the *airport*," Colette suggested. "Maybe someone saw him!"

"I don't know what to do," Nicky said in frustration. "What if we go to Istanbul but he's still here in Hierapolis? I'm not convinced he really went back to **ISTANBUL** without telling us."

"We can divide up into two groups,"

Violet proposed. "Colette and Paulina will go to Istanbul, while Nicky, Pam, and I do some investigating around here. Sound good?"

Kamil offered to give Colette and Paulina a ride to the *airport*, and they took off in a hurry.

Hmmm . . . Have you seen this mouse?

Luckily, they had taken many photos during their trip to Hierapolis. So they showed Akhun's photo to everyone working at the airport, hoping someone had seen **their friend** the night before. But most of the mice they spoke with hadn't been at work the previous evening, and no one recalled seeing Akhun at any other time, either.

"Now what?" asked Paulina, feeling a little disheartened.

Colette pointed to a **SIGN** in the window of a restaurant just outside the airport terminal. It read:

Fly to Istanbul immediately!

The advertisement was for a local airline company that specialized in last-minute flights.

"Well, since we haven't found anything here, we could go to Akhun's family's house in Istanbul and check on him there," Colette pointed out.

So Colette and Paulina bought tickets and got on the first plane they could. During the FLIGHT, they studied the map of Istanbul and located the neighborhood where their friend lived.

Once they landed, they headed straight for a taxi stand. A few moments later they were in a car heading toward . . .

Akhun's family's house!

mint TEA . . . AND MORE QUESTIONS!

As Paulina and Colette got out of the taxi in front of Akhun's family's house, a mouse exited and began heading away from them. From the back, the mouse looked just like their friend!

"Akhun!" Colette exclaimed.

The mouse turned, a perplexed look on his snout. Colette took a closer look and realized it wasn't Akhun. This mouse was a little shorter, had longer hair, and seemed a few years younger.

"Hi," the mouse said, smiling. "I'm Omer. I think you must be looking for my brother."

"Wow!" Paulina exclaimed. "You two really look ALiKE!"

Omer laughed.

"Yes, everyone tells me that," he replied, running a paw through his hair. "If you're looking for Akhun, I'm afraid I have **bad news**."

"Oh, really?" Colette asked casually.

"He's not here," Omer continued.

"Ah, do you know **where** he is?" Paulina asked.

"In Hierapolis," Omer replied. "He's working on an **archaeological** expedition there."

The mouselets exchanged a look: They didn't want to **SQUEAK** too much because they were afraid of worrying Omer.

"Ah, that's too

We're looking for Akhun!

He's in Hierapolis!

bad," Colette said with a sigh. "We really *wanted* to see him!"

"Yes, we're here on vacation," Paulina added. "We met him in an **international** archaeology course, and we were hoping he'd be home so we could say a **QUICK** hello."

A middle-aged gentlemouse **came out** of the house.

Welcome!

"Omer, weren't you leaving?" he asked.

"Dad, I want to introduce you to Akhun's **friends**," Omer replied. "They came to say hi. They didn't know he was in Hierapolis."

Colette and Paulina **LOOKED** at Akhun's father from head to tail. He seemed to be in great shape, without any signs of a bicycle **ACCIDENT**.

"Oh, that's too bad!" responded the man.

"But didn't you try to Call him before coming here?"

"We wanted to surprise him," Colette said.

"Ah, I understand," he replied. "I'm really SORRY that you came here for nothing. Can I at least offer you some mint tea?"

Colette and Paulina did not want to be

rude. They **ACCEPTED** the invitation and headed inside, where they met Akhun's mom.

As they enjoyed some delicious mint tea and almond cookies, Paulina and Colette heard all about Akhun and how **PROUD** his family was of his accomplishments. He had decided as a young mouselet to become an **archaeologist**, and he had showed great dedication and worked hard to follow his passion.

He's not here!

Akhun's mom showed them PHOTOS of their son as a child at the archaeology museum, happy among the ancient artifacts.

The mouselets thanked Akhun's parents and took another taxi back to the airport.

Before they boarded their flight back to Hierapolis, Colette called Nicky.

"Akhun isn't in **ISTANBUL**," Colette said quickly. "And his father definitely did not have a bicycle accident . . . something StRaNGe is going on!"

CLUE!

WHY WOULD AKHUN SEND THAT TEXT IF HIS FATHER WAS FINE AND HE NEVER WENT TO ISTANBUL? WHAT'S GOING ON?

HAVE YOU SEEN THIS MOUSE?

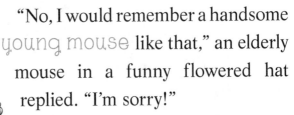

I haven't seen him.

In the meantime, Nicky, Violet, and Pam had been walking all around Hierapolis, Showing Akhun's photo to every tourist they met.

"No, I'm sorry," said a thin gentleman with red hair. "I haven't seen him."

I'm sorry!

"No, I would remember a handsome young mouse like that," an elderly mouse in a funny flowered hat replied. "I'm sorry!"

Everyone else they asked had the same reply: No one had seen their FRIEND.

Nicky sighed, feeling disheartened.

"We've been **SQUEAKING** with mice all day long and we haven't even found a single clue about where Akhun went!" she lamented. "And why did he send that *message* to the professor if it wasn't **TRUE**?"

"Maybe he is **hiding** something from us," Violet suggested.

"But what?" Nicky asked, perplexed. "He seemed so sincere! I don't know him well, but I can't believe he would leave like this, out of the blue, without giving us an explanation."

"You're right," Pam agreed with a nod. "I'm afraid something unexpected must have **happened** to him."

"I have an idea!" Violet squeaked suddenly. "We can go to speak with Professor Brenninger and his team! They're the **only ones** we haven't talked to yet."

"But they were at dinner with us," Pam pointed out. "How would they have any information?"

"Akhun could have DISAPPEARED before dinner," Nicky noted. "Remember, the last time his roommates saw Akhun they were all getting ready to go out."

"And Professor Brenninger, Carl, or Sandra might have run into him at another point in the evening," Violet added. "Any CLUe would help us, no matter how SMALL!"

So Nicky, Violet, and Pam headed toward Professor Brenninger's tent.

Would you like an autograph?

"What can I do for you three?" Professor Brenninger asked. "Do you want an autograph? Or a photo with the most talented archaeologist of our time?"

"Ahem, no," Violet said. "Actually,

we're looking for our friend **Akhun**. He didn't show up to the dinner last night, and no one has seen him."

"Well, he missed a FANTASTIC meal!" Brenninger replied, shaking his snout. "His loss, I'm afraid. But I'm sure he's around here somewhere. Now if you'll excuse me —"

"Professor, please," Nicky interrupted. "We're **WORRIED**. It's not like him to disappear like this. Maybe you or one of your team members saw him before he disappeared? Or maybe you saw something that might be a small clue . . ."

"I'm sorry," Professor Brenninger said, quickly brushing her off. "But I haven't seen your friend, and I don't have **TIME** to spend worrying about where he might be! I'm sure he just wandered off and forgot to fill you in on where he was going."

At that moment, Carl arrived. As he hopped out of his car, **something** fell from his pocket. It was a CELL PHONE.

Nicky bent down to pick it up, but Carl was quicker.

"It's mine!" he snarled at her as he grabbed the phone and quickly slipped it back into his pocket.

Huh?!

A cell phone?

It's mine!

A REVEALING CLUE

Nicky took a step back from Carl, astonished at his strange reaction.

"I'm sorry," she squeaked. "I know it's yours! I was just trying to **help**."

Professor Brenninger appeared suddenly.

"Please excuse Carl," he explained. "He tends to overreact at times. Now shouldn't you be getting back to your work with Professor Buruk?"

With those words, the professor kindly but firmly escorted Nicky, Violet, and Pam toward their excavation site.

"Keep your chin up," Violet told Nicky, who was looking even more dejected than she had earlier.

"There's still ONE THING we can do:

Let's look for clues at the excavation site. Maybe we can find a useful clue in the **canteen tent** or the tool shed.

"That seems pretty unlikely to me," Nicky replied, **discouraged**.

"Well, it's worth a try!" Pamela agreed. "And then we need to speak with the professor."

Nicky, though, was **DUBIOUS**.

"I . . . I don't want to get Akhun in trouble," she said. "From what we've discovered so far, it seems likely he **went away** for some reason he kept secret. And we know he didn't tell Professor Buruk the truth. It still feels **ALL WRONG** to me, but I want to trust Akhun!"

Violet put her arm around her friend.

"I understand why you don't want to inform Professor Buruk," she said kindly. "But we really have to. He oversees the excavation, and it's important that he knows what's **GOING ON**!"

Nicky sighed.

"I know," she said. "But if you don't mind, first I'd like to take a *quick walk* to clear my head."

"No problem!" Pam replied. "In the meantime, Violet and I will take a last look around. Then the three of us can speak with Professor Buruk all together."

While Nicky went on her way, Violet and Pam returned to the excavation site. They scoured all the communal spaces but found nothing. Then they bumped into Alya. She was busy returning some tools to the storage shed.

"Can we come in?" Pam asked hesitantly.

"Why?" Alya replied SUSPICIOUSLY.

"We're looking for Akhun," Violet replied.

"And you think you're going to find him here?" Alya said with a little laugh.

"No, but maybe there's some **CLUE** in there that could be helpful," Violet explained.

Alya shrugged and stepped aside to let them **ENTER**.

"Suit yourselves," she responded. "But I don't think you'll find anything in here."

Violet and Pam **looked** around. It seemed that everything was in its place, but Pam spotted a strange sparkly object on the floor, right under the window.

"What is it?" Violet asked as Pam bent

down to pick up the item.

"I don't know where Akhun went, but I THiNK I solved another mystery," she replied, showing Pam and Alya the object.

The other two girls came closer.

"An earring?" Alya asked, perplexed.

Violet let out a little yelp.

"I think I know who this earring belongs to!" she exclaimed. "It's Brenninger's assistant Sandra's! I saw it on her when she ARRIVED."

Alya took out her cell phone and began flipping through her PHOTOS from the dinner with Professor Brenninger and his assistants.

"Look," Alya said. "She isn't wearing it in this photo."

"Do you know what this means?" Pam

asked. "She must have LOST this earring before the dinner. And what happened here a few days before the dinner?"

Alya blanched.

"So our equipment really was Stolen!" she squeaked in disbelief. "We must tell Professor Buruk immediately!"

CLUE!

AKHUN MYSTERIOUSLY DISAPPEARED RIGHT AFTER PROFESSOR BRENNINGER AND HIS TEAM MADE AN IMPORTANT DISCOVERY. AND NOW VIOLET AND PAM FOUND SANDRA'S EARRING IN THE EQUIPMENT SHED!

A MEETING AMONG THE RUINS

Meanwhile, Nicky was walking among the ruins of Hierapolis with no idea as to what her friends had just discovered.

Maybe Akhun left because he just wasn't interested in the excavation anymore, Nicky thought to herself. But then she shook her head.

"No," she said aloud. "That's just not POSSIBLE."

Suddenly, she noticed a young tourist wandering the ruins, a worried look on her snout.

"Muffin!" she called. "Muffin! Where are you? **HERE, GIRL!** Here, Muffin!"

Nicky approached the young mouse.

"What's wrong?" she asked.

The mouselet looked at her desolately.

"My puppy Muffin got out of her carrier," she said anxiously. "I was DISTRACTED for a second, and now I can't find her anywhere!"

What's wrong?

I lost my dog!

"I'll help you look," Nicky offered. Together they **wandered** into an area of the ruins Nicky hadn't explored before.

"Muffin!" Nicky called. "Come here, girl! Your friend is LOOKING for you!"

Suddenly, she saw a flash of fur among the dusty ruins. Then she heard a small dog howl.

"I found her!" Nicky squeaked, pointing at the dog. Muffin was sniffing around an **old stone ruin** and barking excitedly.

When her owner called her, Muffin trotted right to her as if **nothing** had happened.

"Oh, Muffin, you **scared** me! I thought you were **lost!**" the mouselet said as she squeezed the puppy close. Then she **TURNED** to Nicky. "Thank you so much! I don't know what I would have done without your **HELP**."

Nicky gave Muffin a pat and said good-bye to both of them. Then she decided to go see what Muffin had been sniffing near the **old stone ruin** . . .

A CRY FOR HELP

Nicky **WALKED** toward the ruin carefully. As she got closer to the ancient stone structure, she heard a **strange** hiss. She was just pawsteps away when the hiss **TRANSFORMED** into a voice.

"Help!" someone whispered from inside the ruin.

Nicky **RAN** the last few steps until she was just outside the crumbling building.

"Be careful!" whispered the voice urgently. "Don't come in!"

Nicky stopped at the door. She noticed right away that there was no **floor** inside the structure. Instead, there was a large hole in the ground. The building must have once had two **stories**, but with the passage of time, it was half-covered over with dirt.

Nicky carefully peered inside, hoping to catch a glimpse of the mouse down below. Once her **eyes** got used to the darkness, they met two other dark eyes **staring** back from below.

"Akhun!" Nicky exclaimed happily.

"Nicky!" Akhun replied in a hoarse whisper. "Thank goodmouse you found me. I knew I could count on you. Can you hear me? I've been yelling help all day and I lost my squeak!"

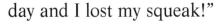

"I can hear you," Nicky replied. "But how did you get DOWN there?"

"It was **Brenninger** and his assistant **Carl**!" Akhun replied.

"Professor Brenninger?!"

Nicky exclaimed in shock. "Why would he do such a thing?"

"If you can help pull me out, I'll explain," Akhun squeaked.

"How do I do that?" Nicky asked, worried. Surely, Akhun was too **HEAVY** for her to lift by his arms.

"There is a LADDER outside," Akhun replied. "I used it to get down here."

Nicky hurried to look for the ladder. She scrambled around the **ancient ruin**, searching high and low. Finally, she found a rusty old metal ladder. She carried it back to Akhun and gently placed it down into the hole where he was trapped. A minute later, her friend had **CLIMBED** out.

Nicky was so happy to see him safe and sound that she threw her arms around his neck in a hug.

"Hey, you're strangling me!" Akhun laughed. But he looked relieved, too.

"We searched all day for you!" Nicky cried. "I'm so glad I found you. Now, **what happened**?"

"It was **Brenninger**," Akhun replied. "When he announced his *discovery* of the two statues, I was feeling a little down. We had been digging for months, and then **another** archaeologist arrived and made the discovery of the century just a week later! I know this work requires great **patience**, but I was so **FRUSTRATED**!"

Nicky smiled at him understandingly. Akhun passed his paw through his hair and continued.

"So I decided to take a **walk** to clear my head, and I found this place. I climbed down the ladder to EXPLORE. While I was down there, I heard voices overhead. No one could see me, but I heard Professor Brenninger and Carl talking about the statues. It turns out the professor is a **fraud**, and the statues are **fake**! I began climbing up to **CONFRONT** them, but that's when they found me.

"Carl quickly climbed down and took my phone so I couldn't call for help. Then he scrambled back up and took the ladder before I could **FOLLOW**! At least they left me some food and water."

Nicky was **shocked**.

"How awful!" she exclaimed. "So that's how they sent that message to Professor Buruk from your phone. What a **dirty** trick! We have to tell Professor Buruk **RIGHT AWAY**!"

WHAT now?

While Nicky was rescuing Akhun, Violet, Pam, and Alya were speaking with Professor Buruk. They showed him the earring they had found and explained what they believed had happened.

"Are you really sure this earring belongs to Sandra?" the professor asked. "We don't want to accuse her of something so serious unless we are positive."

Violet nodded.

"I'm sure I saw her wearing it," she said. "And why else would her earring be in our **EQUIPMENT SHED**?

"Think about it, Professor," she added. "If someone wanted to simply STEAL the tools, why would they leave them in the tower ruins?

This isn't a theft — it's **sabotage**!"

"She's right!" Alya exclaimed.

The professor looked at her with wonder.

"I see you're finally working together with these mice on something, Alya," he said, smiling. "I'm **proud** of your excellent teamwork."

But then the professor shook his head dejectedly.

"But what can I do?" he squeaked helplessly. "It all looks suspicious, but unfortunately it isn't proof of any **wrongdoing**. And I don't understand why Professor Brenninger and his assistants would do something like this."

"I'll explain **why**!" Akhun announced, throwing open the door. His **squeak** was back, and his words made everyone **JUMP** in their seats.

"Akhun!" Professor Buruk said in surprise. "I thought you were in **ISTANBUL** taking care of your father after his bicycle accident! You sent me a **message** to say that's where you had gone."

"It wasn't Akhun who **sent** that message," Nicky explained. She had been right behind Akhun. "It was **Carl**! He stole Akhun's cell phone after he and Professor Brenninger

trapped Akhun in the pit of an old ruin!"

"That makes **sense**!" Violet exclaimed. "That's why Carl reacted so possessively when that cell phone fell out of his pocket!"

"That's right," Pam confirmed, nodding. "He hid it because he was **SCARED** that we would realize it was Akhun's!"

"But why did Professor Brenninger and his assistants FABRICATE all this?" asked Professor Buruk in surprise. "First they sabotaged our excavation by taking our tools, and then they stole Akhun's phone and trapped him. But why?!"

"I think they wanted to create a diversion, Professor," Nicky suggested. "They were looking for ways to distract us and keep us **BUSY** so we wouldn't uncover the truth."

"The truth about what?" Professor Buruk asked, perplexed. He still looked completely

lost. "Please don't keep me in suspense: Tell me **everything**!"

Akhun nodded.

"Professor, the truth is that the statues Brenninger found are **FAKES**!" Akhun replied. "I overheard him and Carl talking about their **DECEPTION**. That's why they trapped me in the ruin: They didn't want me

to interfere with the announcement of their great DISCOVERY!"

Professor jumped up.

"We must stop them!" he exclaimed.

Violet looked at the clock.

"His press conference begins in Denizli in half an hour," she said. "If we leave now we can make it. There's no time to lose!"

OPERATION: STOP BRENNINGER!

As Violet, Nicky, and Pam rushed out of Professor Buruk's cabin, followed by Alya, Colette and Paulina were just ARRIVING back in Hierapolis.

You're back!

Hooray!

"Hi!" they greeted their friends warmly. Then they saw Akhun and ran to **HUG** him. "Where have you **BEEN**?!" Colette asked.

"We were so worried!" Paulina added. "We went all

the way to **ISTANBUL** to try to find you!"

"It's been quite a day," Colette added. She looked **exhausted**. "We took a last-minute flight and went there and back in just a few hours. I'm glad for a break from **RUSHING** around!"

"Sorry, but your **BREAK** is going to have to wait," Nicky told her friend. "We're on our way to Denizli right now, and we have to *hurry*!"

"What?" Colette asked, perplexed. "Why?"

"Brenninger's statues are **FAKE**!" Pam explained quickly. "Akhun discovered the scam, and Brenninger and Carl trapped him in some ancient ruins. Luckily, Nicky found him. We're on our way to Brenninger's press conference right now to **expose** him!"

"All aboard!" Professor Buruk called as he pulled up in the team's van. "We'll explain everything better during the ride.

"We must get to the university in Denizli right away. That's where Brenninger is about to speak about his **FAKE** discovery."

Pam, Violet, and Nicky told Colette and Paulina the entire story as Professor Buruk navigated through **traffic**.

"We must expose him in front of the whole world," the professor said. "We can't let him **discredit** the good name of archaeology."

Alya glanced at her watch.

"The press conference is about to begin!" she squeaked. "We'll **NEVER** make it in time!"

A small **traffic jam** was building just ahead of them. Two tourists with a map in hand had stopped a taxi driver to ask for **directions**. The driver had turned to a bus driver for help, and now the two were **consulting** each other in the middle of the street.

Akhun **POINTED** at a side street.

"Go that way, Professor!" he said. "I know another way!"

Professor Buruk did as Akhun suggested and took one street after another, finally pulling up right in front of the university.

"**Great job!**" Alya exclaimed, patting Akhun's shoulder.

Everyone **looked** at her, astonished at her unusual outburst. She smiled and pulled back her paw, looking a bit embarrassed.

"Okay, let's go!" Professor Buruk exclaimed as he parked the **minivan** and turned off the ignition.

The group ran straight toward the entrance to the university.

At the door, a **THREATENING-LOOKING** security rat dressed in a black suit stopped them.

"*PLEASE*, we need to get inside right away!" Professor Buruk explained. "We have **important** information to share with the press!"

The mouse shook his head.

"**I'M SORRY**, but the press conference has already begun," he said. "I've been instructed not to allow **anyone** to enter late."

CONFRONTING
THE IMPOSTER

Professor Buruk stepped up to the rat with confidence.

"Excuse me, but I am a colleague of Professor Brenninger," he said. "I was stuck in traffic, but it's very **IMPORTANT** for me to get to the press conference."

"Okay, I can let you in," the guard replied. "But just you."

"These are my students," Professor Buruk said. "They are talented, passionate young archaeologists, and they'll never have another opportunity to meet a mouse like Professor Brenninger."

"Let's hope that's true!" Akhun muttered under his breath.

"Oh, fine," the guard said at last. "If it means that much to you all, go in. But please be quiet when you enter."

The guard moved ASIDE to let them pass. The room was full of journalists. Brenninger had already begun squeaking at the podium in front of the room.

"Now what do we do, Professor?" Akhun asked softly. He was a little intimidated.

"Now we reveal the truth," Professor Buruk whispered back. Then he cleared his throat and spoke loudly, so the entire room could hear.

"That man is an imposter!" he cried. "The statues are FAKES!"

"What?!" cried a few of the journalists, as they turned and began snapping Professor Buruk's PHOTO.

Professor Buruk moved toward the podium

at the front of the room, followed by the Thea Sisters, Alya, and Akhun.

"Don't listen to these amateurs!" Professor Brenninger shouted. "They're lying! They're just jealous because I made an important discovery and they didn't."

"This man is the liar," Akhun replied. "He locked me in a ruin to stop me from revealing the truth: These statues are fake!"

Two policemice ran into the room, accompanied by the guard who had let Professor Buruk and his team into the press conference. He had a furious look on his snout.

"Arrest them!" yelled Brenninger.

"No, arrest him!" Akhun replied, pointing at Brenninger. "He's an **imposter** and a mousenapper!"

The police seemed perplexed, while the journalists continued taking notes, snapping PHOTOS, and whispering urgently to one another.

Brenninger glanced around. Seeing that things weren't going well, he tried to take advantage of the confusion in the room by making a sudden dash for the EMERGENCY EXIT.

THE SCAM IS UNVEILED

Luckily, Nicky saw Brenninger's escape.

"He's getting away!" she exclaimed as she sprinted after him, followed by the other Thea Sisters.

Brenninger had run out of the building, and the Thea Sisters followed him through the streets of the city.

"Stop!" yelled Colette.

"Never!" Brenninger replied.

He tried to slow down the Thea Sisters by knocking things into their path, including a basket of pomegranates from a fruit stall on the street.

"Hey! What are you doing?!" the fruit seller cried, waving his paw threateningly at

Brenninger as he scampered by.

"Come on, Brenninger!" Nicky shouted at the mouse. "**GIVE UP!** Everyone knows now that the statues are **FAKE**!"

"You'll never catch me!" came Brenninger's reply. "**NO ONE** can stop me!"

And as he said this, he turned a corner and ran right into the two policemice, who had taken a different street.

The Thea Sisters got permission to speak with Brenninger before he was TAKEN to the police station.

You'll never catch me!

Hey!

"Why did you do it?" Nicky asked.

For a moment, it seemed Brenninger was going to brush her off with one of his typical RUDE responses. But then he changed his mind.

"Do you remember what I told you about the PRESTIGIOUS universities where I worked?" he asked.

The Thea Sisters nodded.

"Well, I don't work for them anymore," he said. "They fired me because they didn't believe in my abilities. So I thought if I made a great discovery, they would give me another chance."

"But your discovery is a FAKE," Colette said. "Didn't you realize someone would expose you?"

"I was sure everyone would BELIEVE me," he said with a shrug. "And I would have gotten away with it, too, if it hadn't been for you snoops!"

The police **took** Brenninger to the police station, and they asked the Thea Sisters, Professor Buruk, Akhun, and Alya to drop by as well to leave witness statements. As they were exiting the station after giving their testimonies, the Thea Sisters bumped right into the **fruit seller** whose fruit Brenninger had knocked over.

"I remember you!" the man said. "What happened to that mouse you were **chasing**? He ruined my **pomegranates** and cost me a lot of money."

The Thea Sisters explained what had happened to Brenninger. Then they went with the man to his stall to see if they could help make things **RIGHT**.

"We'll pick you up there," Professor Buruk told them, and he, Akhun, and Alya went to get the minivan.

THE RETURN TO HIERAPOLIS

After the Thea Sisters' visit to the fruit stall, the group finally headed back to Hierapolis as the sun began to set.

Colette held a paper bag in her lap as she retold the story of how she and the others CHASED Brenninger through the streets of Istanbul.

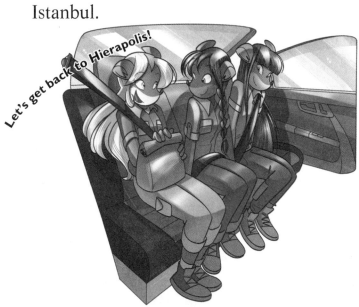

Let's get back to Hierapolis!

"Carl and Sandra were arrested immediately, too," Akhun added. He hadn't had a chance to tell the Thea Sisters what happened after they left. "The police quickly discovered that they were FAKE archaeologists. And Carl still had my CELL PHONE in his pocket!"

"And all those incidents at the campsite were meant to be distractions to keep us from noticing that the statues weren't real!" Alya said, shaking her head in dismay.

"All's well that ends well!" Professor Buruk chimed in from the driver's seat. "I'm only sorry you students had your work experience on the dig interrupted by this misadventure."

"But it's not your fault, Professor!" Nicky exclaimed. "And we've learned so much from our work on the site and from these unexpected events.

"We know now that successful **archaeologists** work and study hard, are patient and dedicated, and aren't AFRAID of getting dirty!"

"And we also know how important it is to work as a team and not go looking for shortcuts!" Violet added.

"Well, then I would say that not eVeRYTHING went wrong," Professor Buruk said with a SMILE. "You five have been excellent assistants!"

"It's too bad it's almost time to go home," Pam said with a sigh. "But at least we resolved the RIDDLE of the ruins!"

"Only one mystery remains," Alya said thoughtfully.

"What is it?" asked Paulina, a PUZZLED look on her snout.

"The mystery of what's in that paper

bag," Alya replied, pointing at Colette's lap.

Colette laughed. "These are the pomegranates I bought from Mr. Aziz's fruit stall," she explained. "He was upset that Brenninger had **ruined** so much of his fruit, so we decided to buy some for the entire team to share."

"I love pomegranates!" Alya exclaimed.

"They're my favorite fruit! I can show you all how to make a delicious pomegranate juice."

"That would be great!" Colette replied, smiling.

Alya smiled back.

A moment later, the minivan arrived at the excavation site and the mice all piled out.

"I'm sorry I was so mean to you when you first arrived," Alya told the Thea Sisters with a sigh. "I didn't realize how great you were! I shouldn't have JUDGED you before getting to know you."

In reply, the Thea Sisters pulled her into a group hug. They were happy to have a new friend!

GOOD-BYE, TURKEY!

The next day, Professor Buruk organized a party to say good-bye to the Thea Sisters, who would be *leaving* the following day.

The whole team got to work to make the last night in Hierapolis **unforgettable**. Professor Buruk revealed that he was a great **COOK**, and he prepared some Turkish specialties, including *dolma* — grape leaves stuffed with rice.

"Everything is delicious!" Colette exclaimed. "Thanks so much for cooking for us!"

"It is the least I could do," the professor replied.

"You rescued **Akhun** and helped reveal Brenninger as a fraud. I'm **grateful** for everything you've done to contribute to our team and to our important **archaeological** work!"

"Would anyone like a little pomegranate juice?" Alya asked as she offered around a tray of glasses of **brilliant-colored** red juice.

"Thanks!" Violet replied as she grabbed a glass. The others followed.

"I propose a **toast**!" said Professor Buruk. "To the exceptional Mouseford students: We were honored to have you work with us. I know you will go on to do **great things**, whether it is in the field of **archaeology** or along another path!"

Everyone came **together** to toast the Thea Sisters, including Alya and Akhun.

"I'm **SAD** to see you all go," Akhun said to Nicky.

"Yes, me, too," Nicky replied. "It was really great getting to know you!"

"I imagine you won't forget this **adventure** quickly!" Akhun said with a laugh. "And I won't, either! Without you, I would still be in that **hole**! Write to me the next time you're in Istanbul. You and your friends are always **welcome** to stay with my family."

"That's such a nice offer, **thanks**!" Nicky replied.

Come visit me in Istanbul!

"And if one day we both become **archaeologists**, maybe we'll cross paths at the same excavation site," Akhun added, his eyes shining **HAPPILY**. "But for now let's put on some **MUSIC** and dance!"

And with that, Akhun

turned on a radio, and he and Alya danced with their new friends the Thea Sisters until the **SUN** had set over the ruins of Hierapolis.

THEY WERE MORE THAN FRIENDS. THEY WERE SISTERS!

Thea Sisters

Don't miss any of these exciting Thea Sisters adventures!

Thea Stilton and the Dragon's Code

Thea Stilton and the Mountain of Fire

Thea Stilton and the Ghost of the Shipwreck

Thea Stilton and the Secret City

Thea Stilton and the Mystery in Paris

Thea Stilton and the Cherry Blossom Adventure

Thea Stilton and the Star Castaways

Thea Stilton: Big Trouble in the Big Apple

Thea Stilton and the Ice Treasure

Thea Stilton and the Secret of the Old Castle

Thea Stilton and the Blue Scarab Hunt

Thea Stilton and the Prince's Emerald

Thea Stilton and the Mystery on the Orient Express

Thea Stilton and the Dancing Shadows

Thea Stilton and the Legend of the Fire Flowers

Thea Stilton and the Spanish Dance Mission

Thea Stilton and the Journey to the Lion's Den

Thea Stilton and the Great Tulip Heist

Thea Stilton and the Chocolate Sabotage

Thea Stilton and the Missing Myth

Thea Stilton and the Lost Letters

Thea Stilton and the Tropical Treasure

Thea Stilton and the Hollywood Hoax

Thea Stilton and the Madagascar Madness

Thea Stilton and the Frozen Fiasco

Thea Stilton and the Venice Masquerade

Thea Stilton and the Niagara Splash

Thea Stilton and the Riddle of the Ruins

Up Next!

Thea Stilton and the Phantom of the Orchestra

And check out my fabumouse special editions!

THEA STILTON:
THE JOURNEY
TO ATLANTIS

THEA STILTON:
THE SECRET OF
THE FAIRIES

THEA STILTON:
THE SECRET OF
THE SNOW

THEA STILTON:
THE CLOUD
CASTLE

THEA STILTON:
THE TREASURE
OF THE SEA

THEA STILTON:
THE LAND OF
FLOWERS

THEA STILTON:
THE SECRET OF THE
CRYSTAL FAIRIES

Be sure to read all my fabumouse adventures!

#1 Lost Treasure of the Emerald Eye

#2 The Curse of the Cheese Pyramid

#3 Cat and Mouse in a Haunted House

#4 I'm Too Fond of My Fur!

#5 Four Mice Deep in the Jungle

#6 Paws Off, Cheddarface!

#7 Red Pizzas for a Blue Count

#8 Attack of the Bandit Cats

#9 A Fabumouse Vacation for Geronimo

#10 All Because of a Cup of Coffee

#11 It's Halloween, You 'Fraidy Mouse!

#12 Merry Christmas, Geronimo!

#13 The Phantom of the Subway

#14 The Temple of the Ruby of Fire

#15 The Mona Mousa Code

#16 A Cheese-Colored Camper

#17 Watch Your Whiskers, Stilton!

#18 Shipwreck on the Pirate Islands

#19 My Name Is Stilton, Geronimo Stilton

#20 Surf's Up, Geronimo!

#21 The Wild, Wild West

#22 The Secret of Cacklefur Castle

A Christmas Tale

#23 Valentine's Day Disaster

#24 Field Trip to Niagara Falls

#25 The Search for Sunken Treasure

#26 The Mummy with No Name

#27 The Christmas Toy Factory

#28 Wedding Crasher

#29 Down and Out Down Under

#30 The Mouse Island Marathon

#31 The Mysterious Cheese Thief

Christmas Catastrophe

#32 Valley of the Giant Skeletons

#33 Geronimo and the Gold Medal Mystery

#34 Geronimo Stilton, Secret Agent

#35 A Very Merry Christmas

#36 Geronimo's Valentine

#37 The Race Across America

#38 A Fabumouse School Adventure

#39 Singing Sensation

#40 The Karate Mouse

#41 Mighty Mount Kilimanjaro

#42 The Peculiar Pumpkin Thief

#43 I'm Not a Supermouse!

#44 The Giant Diamond Robbery

#45 Save the White Whale!

#46 The Haunted Castle

#47 Run for the Hills, Geronimo!

#48 The Mystery in Venice

#49 The Way of the Samurai

#50 This Hotel Is Haunted!

#51 The Enormouse Pearl Heist

#52 Mouse in Space!

#53 Rumble in the Jungle

#54 Get into Gear, Stilton!

#55 The Golden Statue Plot

#56 Flight of the Red Bandit

#57 The Stinky Cheese Vacation

#58 The Super Chef Contest

#59 Welcome to Moldy Manor

#60 The Treasure of Easter Island

#61 Mouse House Hunter

#62 Mouse Overboard!

#63 The Cheese Experiment

#64 Magical Mission

#65 Bollywood Burglary

#66 Operation: Secret Recipe

#67 The Chocolate Chase

#68 Cyber-Thief Showdown

#69 Hug a Tree, Geronimo

Up Next!

#70 The Phantom Bandit

THANKS FOR READING, AND GOOD-BYE UNTIL OUR NEXT ADVENTURE!

TheaSisters